Shadow
Squadron

SHADOW
SQUADRON

GUARDIAN ANGEL

STONE ARCH BOOKS
a capstone imprint

SHADOW
SQUADRON

GUARDIAN ANGEL

WRITTEN BY
CARL BOWEN

ILLUSTRATED BY
WILSON TORTOSA

AND
BENNY FUENTES

COVER ART BY
MARC LEE

Shadow Squadron is published by
Stone Arch Books,
A Capstone Imprint,
1710 Roe Crest Drive
North Mankato, MN 56003
www.capstonepub.com

Cataloging-in-Publication Data is available on the
Library of Congress website.

ISBN: 978-1-4965-0382-4 (library binding)
ISBN: 978-1-4965-0386-2 (paperback)

Summary: Shadow Squadron has a new team
member, and he is welcomed with their most
challenging mission yet. The Secretary of State has
been kidnapped in the Central African Republic by
child soldiers. Unwilling to harm the armed youths,
Lieutenant Commander Ryan Cross will have to get
creative and stretch his resources to the limits if he
wants to save the Secretary.

Printed in China
1215/201501675
112015 009346R

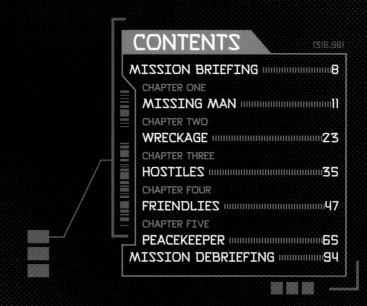

CONTENTS

1316.981

2012.101

ACCESS GRANTED

SHADOW SQUADRON DOSSIER

CROSS, RYAN

RANK: Lieutenant Commander
BRANCH: Navy SEAL
PSYCH PROFILE: Cross is the team leader of Shadow Squadron. Control oriented and loyal, Cross insisted on hand-picking each member of his squad.

PAXTON, ADAM

RANK: Sergeant First Class
BRANCH: Army (Green Beret)
PSYCH PROFILE: Paxton has a knack for filling the role most needed in any team. His loyalty makes him a born second-in-command.

PHOTO NOT AVAILABLE

1216.062

YAMASHITA, KIMIYO

RANK: Lieutenant
BRANCH: Army Ranger
PSYCH PROFILE: The team's sniper is an expert marksman and a true stoic. It seems his emotions are as steady as his trigger finger.

LANCASTER, MORGAN

RANK: Staff Sergeant
BRANCH: Air Force Combat Control
PSYCH PROFILE: The team's newest member is a tech expert who learns fast and has the ability to adapt to any combat situation.

JANNATI, ARAM

PHOTO NOT AVAILABLE

RANK: Second Lieutenant
BRANCH: Army Ranger
PSYCH PROFILE: Jannati serves as the team's linguist. His sharp eyes serve him well as a spotter, and he's usually paired with Yamashita on overwatch.

SHEPHERD, MARK

PHOTO NOT AVAILABLE

RANK: Lieutenant
BRANCH: Army (Green Beret)
PSYCH PROFILE: The heavy-weapons expert of the group, Shepherd's love of combat borders on unhealthy.

2019.681

MISSION BRIEFING

OPERATION

GUARDIAN ANGEL 009

I'd like you all to welcome our newest team member, Heath Rodgers. And please congratulate Adam Paxton as I've decided to promote him in the wake of Chief Walker's departure.

So we have some moving parts, but we can't let that affect the mission at hand. The Secretary of State's chopper has gone done in the Central African Republic, and we've been tapped to save him and any of his travel mates. One last thing: avoid contact with the locals at all costs. The place is a political nightmare, and we do NOT want to get involved in the conflicts.

3245.98 ● ● ●   — Lieutenant Commander Ryan Cross

C.A.R.

PRIMARY OBJECTIVE(S)

- Locate crash site

- Exfiltrate with any survivors

SECONDARY OBJECTIVE(S)

- Avoid contact with locals

1932.789

0412.981

1624.054

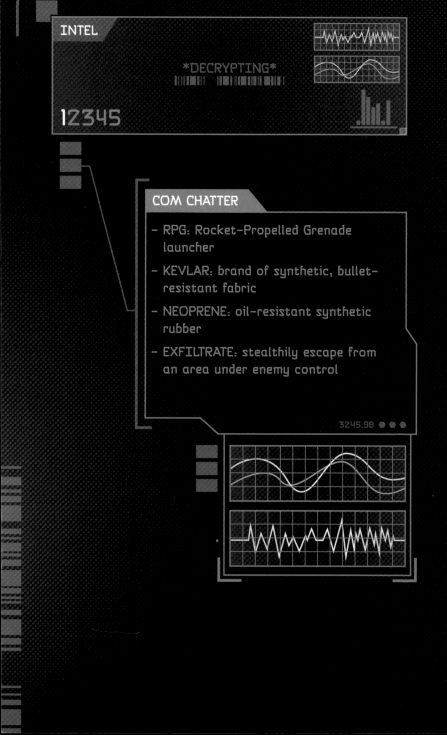

INTEL

DECRYPTING

12345

COM CHATTER

- RPG: Rocket-Propelled Grenade launcher
- KEVLAR: brand of synthetic, bullet-resistant fabric
- NEOPRENE: oil-resistant synthetic rubber
- EXFILTRATE: stealthily escape from an area under enemy control

3245.98

MISSING MAN

"It almost feels unprofessional to be glad one of our planes got shot down," Rodgers said.

Rodgers's commanding officer, Lieutenant Commander Ryan Cross, couldn't help but grin. He and his team's newest member, Gunnery Sergeant Heath Rodgers, had gotten along famously ever since Rodgers arrived from the Marine Special Operations Regiment. From his early interviews with Cross and through the weeks of cohesion training with Cross's team, Rodgers had proven himself easygoing, competent, and agreeable. Cross appreciated those qualities more than he could say.

Rodgers's service record was exemplary, but that went without saying. Shadow Squadron settled for nothing but the best. The top-secret special-missions unit consisted of elite soldiers from the Navy SEALs, Green Berets, Army Rangers, Air Force Combat Controllers, and Marine Special Operations Regiment.

The team had traveled all over the world whenever the US government had an interest in military intervention but couldn't act openly.

Shadow Squadron had enjoyed many victories as a result of the team's superior training and access to cutting-edge gear. The team also suffered its share of losses, including their first fatality during a rescue mission in the Gulf of Mexico. And a counter-sniper operation in Iraq had almost cost one soldier his life and integrity.

The team recently lost its tech specialist to another job. Those who remained on the team had suffered through everything from gunshot wounds to frostbite.

Yet the worst heartache had hit during the team's

last mission. A CIA agent had proven himself a traitor to his agency and his country. Shadow Squadron exposed the agent's twisted scheme to defraud the government out of millions of dollars by taking advantage of the War on Terror. The man had even ordered a bombing that severely wounded Cross's second-in-command, Chief Petty Officer Alonso Walker.

Walker's injuries proved to be career-ending. At first, Command urged Cross to fill Walker's spot on the team with Rodgers. Instead, Cross insisted on promoting from within. Command eventually agreed, awarding Green Beret Adam Paxton a long-overdue promotion from Staff Sergeant to Sergeant First Class.

Paxton reluctantly stepped up to take the second-in-command position. Rodgers took Paxton's place. Rodgers didn't utter a single complaint, even though Cross had put Paxton ahead of him in line, which was yet another point in Rodgers's favor. The Marine understood that Cross had done so because it was best for the team, and Rodgers completely respected that. And for that, Cross respected Rodgers.

And it didn't hurt that Rodgers could make Cross laugh. No one else on the team was particularly good at that.

* * *

Shadow Squadron's temporary base of operations was an empty, corrugated-metal hangar on an abandoned airstrip. The building was located in the middle of the Adamawa Region of Cameroon in Africa.

For three weeks, the team had been hunting the members of an elusive extremist militant group called Boko Haram. Though small in scale, it had plagued officials in Nigeria since the turn of the century. It had even earned an official designation as a terrorist organization from the US government.

The group's leader had been wounded in a firefight with Nigerian troops. He was presumed dead, but US intelligence analysts were convinced that he'd taken refuge in Cameroon instead.

"All right, listen up," Cross said. The other seven soldiers in Shadow Squadron were seated before him, on whatever boxes or barrels they could find. "An emergency call has just come in from Command. This game of hide-and-seek we're playing has to be put on hold."

"That's a shame, sir," Sergeant Mark Shepherd said, grinning like a kid. "I got a good lead yesterday on where we can find Elvis."

Shepherd, a Green Beret like Paxton, had eased into the role of class clown after the team's previous joker, Edgar Brighton, left. Ever since Chief Walker had been taken out of action, Shepherd took the job very seriously. He seemed to think that maintaining the group's morale was his sole responsibility. Cross suspected that Shepherd made his jokes mostly to uplift his own mood.

Either way, Cross allowed it — to a point.

"Elvis is old news, man," said Second Lieutenant Aram Jannati, a Marine like Rodgers. "I met a guy last week who swears he saw a UFO chasing a lion."

"Was it Brighton?" Shepherd said.

Chuckles filled the room. Cross could tell his team missed their former colleague's sense of humor.

"Come on, guys," Paxton said. "Can it."

Paxton kept his voice even when he spoke and barely looked up from the tactical pad strapped to his forearm. Unlike Chief Walker, he didn't feel the need to growl or glare when reprimanding others.

"Fortunately we don't have to go far," Cross continued. "This op's a search and recovery mission right next door in the Central African Republic."

CLICK!

Cross tapped the screen of his tactical pad, wirelessly connecting it to a projector on the table. The projector displayed a political map of Africa with a country highlighted in the center.

Cross expanded a similar image on his pad and tapped the highlighted country. The Central African Republic (CAR) and its 16 prefectures appeared.

"A search for what, sir?" Staff Sergeant Morgan Lancaster asked. Lancaster was a USAF combat controller. She'd parachuted into this location a day ahead of the others to ready the site for their arrival.

"A plane," Cross said. "A decommissioned C-130, to be specific. It was chartered by a group of American staff members under the previous ambassador to the CAR. They were thirteen in all, plus a flight crew of two. They had one other person with them, as well. That person is the reason Command called us."

"A politician?" Lieutenant Kimiyo Yamashita asked. Yamashita was an Army Ranger and the team's sniper. His dry tone hinted at a river of doubt beneath the sniper's otherwise steady personality.

"You could say that," Cross said. He brought up an image of a man in a suit.

The team's medic, Hospital Corpsman Second Class Kyle Williams, was the first to speak. "Oh, man," he said. "Tell me that's not our Secretary of State."

"It's him," Paxton confirmed.

"What the heck is he doing here?" Shepherd asked.

"The Secretary was on a secret fact-finding trip to the CAR while heading up a public diplomatic effort to stabilize what's left of this country's government," Cross said. "At some point the night before last, however, he ditched his security detail and boarded a plane with the former ambassador's staffers. They didn't tell anyone where they were going, or why. Whatever the case, the plane was brought down in the bush by an RPG over the Lobaye prefecture. The pilot got one distress call off before the plane crashed but no further communication. We don't know how many survived, nor do we know anything about any local hostile forces."

Cross took a deep breath. He tapped once more on his pad. The device was a little bigger and a lot tougher than an average smartphone. It had a Kevlar and neoprene bracer that held it tightly to the inside of Cross's forearm. At Lancaster's insistence, every member of Shadow Squadron now wore one. While Cross could have simply shared the images from his pad with all the others instead of projecting them on the wall, he didn't like the idea of everyone looking down at their wrists while he was briefing them.

"The pilot panicked when the plane was hit," Cross continued. "Thankfully they didn't come down over any of the major cities. We have enough satellite imagery to know where to start looking. That's going to have to be good enough for us. So here's the plan: we're going to cross the border in the Wraith, find the crash site, search it for survivors, and report in. We'll exfiltrate as many survivors as we can in as few trips as we can. If anyone is missing, we'll run search-and-rescues until we find them."

"Question, sir," Williams said. "What about the current . . . political situation in the country?"

"You mean whose side do we take if we run into a bunch of locals waving guns and machetes around?" Rodgers asked.

"Yeah," Williams said.

"We're not to make contact with the locals," Cross said. "We go in like ghosts, we find our people, and then we get out. If all goes well, no one will ever know we were there except the people who leave along with us."

"Speaking of them," Rodgers said, "I assume the Secretary is our top priority."

"No special treatment," Cross said, though Command had told him the exact opposite. "We have sixteen people missing. That means we have sixteen equal priorities. Is everybody clear on that?"

"Hoo-rah," the rest of the team replied in unison.

INTEL

DECRYPTING
IIIIIIIIII   IIIIIIIIIIIIIIIIIII

12345

COM CHATTER

- CANALPHONE: radio headphone that fits inside the ear

- STEALTH: quiet and sneaky movement

- THERMAL IMAGING: technology that allows the user to see body heat

3245.98 ● ● ●

To put it mildly, the Central African Republic was a mess. It had become a ship at sea in a storm of bloodshed with no one at the helm. Several groups were fighting bloody wars, religious and otherwise, for control and influence.

That was the situation in which Cross found the country as his team stole across the border in the dead of night, looking for sixteen lost Americans.

"I can't stress this enough," Paxton repeated as their helicopter approached their target coordinates. "Absolutely no contact with the locals. Civilian, military, black, white, Christian, Muslim — it doesn't matter. Zero contact. Are we clear?"

"Clear," the team replied in unison — and not for the first time that trip.

"The Wraith's running on fumes," Paxton continued, "so we're not going to have it circling overhead waiting to come scoop us up like we did in Cameroon. While it's gone to refuel, we're completely on our own. I can't stress enough how important stealth is to this mission. Not just to us, but to the people counting on us."

Rodgers looked up from his tactical pad and winked at Cross, as if to say, *He kind of overstressed that point, huh?*

Cross gave Rodgers a barely noticeable smile so Paxton wouldn't see it.

"We're over the site now, Commander," the helicopter pilot reported. "No heat signatures near the wreckage. If there are any survivors, they're not here now."

"Noted," Cross said. "Do you have room to land?"

"The plane cut a swath on its way down, but it's not wide enough."

"Just get us over the wreckage then," Cross said. "We'll drop in."

"You got it, Commander."

"All right, listen up," Cross said to his soldiers. "We're over the crash site, but nobody's waiting for us. We're going to fast-rope down and hoof it until the Wraith gets back. Look sharp, watch out for each other, and remember what we said about the locals."

"No contact," Paxton said again, as if it were the first time.

"Everybody got that?" Cross said.

"Sir," came the unanimous reply.

"We're ready," Cross told the pilot. "Get the doors open."

* * *

In the light of the half moon, the Wraith descended over the bush. The 65-foot long, eleven ton Wraith had an outer hull designed to deflect and scatter radar signals. The blades of its rotor system were shaped like scythes to reduce the sound they made cutting through the air. It had an internal tail rotor, and its engine was heavily shielded to eliminate engine noise.

The modifications didn't render the helicopter totally silent — no modification could do that. But the Wraith was all but impossible to hear until it was right overhead.

WOOSH WOOSH WOOSH
WOOSH WOOSH WOOSH

When the Wraith arrived at its destination, it hovered quietly over the treetops. The side doors opened, and four thin ropes spooled out the sides.

Seconds later, the members of Cross's team slid down, clipped to the ropes by carabiners. When all eight sets of boots had touched ground, high-speed winches slurped the lines back up like black spaghetti strings.

The Wraith veered away into the night, needing to refuel before it could return to aid in the search and rescue.

Cross took a moment to get accustomed to the night's sticky heat after the cool, conditioned air inside the Wraith. Before him lay the largest intact part of the Secretary of State's wrecked aircraft. It had come down on its back. One wing was missing and only half of the other wing remained. The rudder and tail fin were shredded, and the tail section had been torn almost in half. Jumbled pieces of seats and wiring lay strewn across the ground like the guts of some enormous metal bird's carcass.

Cross signaled Williams and Lancaster to join him. Next, he signaled to Paxton that he wanted a security sweep of the perimeter of the crash site. Paxton nodded. Paxton took Shepherd with him and gestured for Rodgers, Yamashita, and Jannati to move off in the other direction.

As the others fanned out to search the area, Lancaster shrugged off her pack. From it, she produced a black plastic case the size of a lunchbox. She withdrew Four-Eyes, a disc-shaped unmanned aerial vehicle (UAV) designed and built by a departed Shadow Squadron team member.

In the months since her arrival on the team, Lancaster had completely overhauled Four-Eyes'

controls, replacing the bulky dual-stick controller with a single-hand device.

Now, whatever Four-Eyes' cameras saw, Lancaster could project it right into her glasses. All she had to do was shift her eyes a little to see it. With a little tinkering, Lancaster could even use Four-Eyes as a two-way receiver/transmitter like the team's canalphones.

Cross had been intrigued with the improvement, though they'd both agreed that more testing was needed. It couldn't be a distraction on the battlefield.

When Four-Eyes was up and away, Lancaster pinged the transponders in each of the Shadow Squadron's tactical datapads. This gave her a readout of the others' positions relative to herself. She then set the UAV's cameras to thermal imaging and programmed a slow circular flight plan around the crash site. With her teammates' positions already pinged, she could keep an eye out for any other human-sized heat signatures the thermal cameras picked up.

With that done, Lancaster lifted her rifle, stowed Four-Eyes' controller, and gave Cross a thumbs-up.

Cross nodded and led Williams and Lancaster into the wrecked plane. Unsurprisingly, the inside was just as much of a mess as the outside. Every loose object inside the plane had been tossed around like dice in a cup. Much of what was left was broken. There wasn't much left, however. If the plane had been carrying cargo, all of it was gone now.

Williams was the first to find a body. The corpsman knelt beside the still form. Whoever the man had been, he was dead. His neck was broken, and his head hung at an unnatural angle.

Lancaster frowned.

"Perimeter's clear," Paxton said through Cross's canalphone. Since the transmission wasn't addressed specifically to him, the others heard it as well. It was their signal to relax noise discipline.

Cross looked at Lancaster. "What does Four-Eyes see?" he asked.

Lancaster cocked an eyebrow over her glasses. "No heat signatures but ours, sir," she said.

Cross tapped his canalphone. "Reel in," he told the team.

By the time the other five soldiers returned, Cross, Williams, and Lancaster had found six more bodies: four civilians, the pilot, and the copilot. That left nine people unaccounted for, including the Secretary of State.

"There aren't any more bodies within the perimeter," Jannati said. "But we found tire tracks and a lot of footprints. The footprints lead in the direction away from here."

"Probably our survivors," Cross said, mostly to himself.

"Or whoever rode out with the driver loaded their vehicle up with salvage and had to walk back," Paxton said.

"Whoever it was got here pretty soon after the crash," Williams added as he exited the wrecked plane. "There was another body under a tarp that we missed. She'd been shot, once. In the head. She had about two feet of twisted metal speared through her from the crash, though. She would've died from that eventually, but not right away."

"So somebody put her out of her misery?" Rodgers suggested.

"I think so," Williams said.

"Or they knew she'd be more trouble than she was worth as a prisoner," Jannati said. "Especially if she was just going to die anyway."

"Assuming they cared about prisoners," Yamashita added.

"Enough speculating," Cross said. "Eight people are still missing, and there's only one obvious set of tracks leading away from this site. It's the only lead we've got, so let's follow it."

"Sir," his team responded.

INTEL

DECRYPTING

12345

COM CHATTER

- FIRETEAM: small military unit
- M110: artillery shell
- PLANTATION: large piece of land used to grow crops

3245.98

CHAPTER THREE

HOSTILES

From the plane wreckage, the trail hacked a straight line through the underbrush to a rough, unpaved road. The path seemed to have been cleared by hand and was just wide enough for a single vehicle.

Shadow Squadron followed the road in two fireteams under the cover of the trees to either side. Yamashita and Lancaster scouted ahead.

Dawn was still hours away when a click came through in Cross's canalphone. Yamashita reported in from his scouting position up ahead.

"Commander," the sniper said, "we've got something."

Cross signaled for the others to stop. "Go ahead."

"I can see a truck that matches the tracks we've been following. It's parked next to some kind of farmhouse on a hill below us. There's a guard outside it and a few others moving around."

"Do you see any of our people?" Cross asked.

"Commander, I have a good idea where they are," Lancaster answered. "Four-Eyes shows a group of heat signatures in a smaller house down the hill from the first one. It's guarded too."

"We're still half a mile out at the tree line," Yamashita said. "We could get closer."

"Negative," Cross said. "Keep an eye on things, but don't risk being seen. We'll catch up soon."

"Sir. Out."

The team joined up with the scouts a short while later. At the tree line, they met at an outcropping of rock that looked like a nose sticking out of the ground.

Yamashita lay on his stomach halfway up the bridge of the nose. He surveyed the land beyond through the Leupold scope on his M110 sniper rifle. Lancaster lay beside him with her UAV's controller in one hand and a pair of night-vision binoculars in the other. She alternated looking through the binoculars and looking at the readout from Four-Eyes in the prism viewer on her glasses.

When Cross approached, Lancaster met him at the bottom of the rocky slope. When she spoke, her voice sounded hollow. "We've got a problem, Commander," she said. Without explaining further, she handed over the binoculars.

Cross crawled up next to Yamashita and peered through the binoculars. He saw the ground descend sharply in a ridge before leveling out into rolling hills. The entire area was covered with high, green shrubs that bore thick clusters of berries. The shrubs had been planted in even rows, though they looked shaggy and overgrown. The rows between the shrubs were littered with leaves and weedy undergrowth. Cross realized he was looking at an abandoned coffee plantation.

In the center of the plantation, one hill was higher than the others. At its bottom lay a long one-story house with a porch running along the entire front length. Two figures stood on the porch to either side of the door, holding rifles. There was something strange about the two figures holding the guns, but Cross couldn't quite put his finger on why.

At the top of the central hill was another house. This one was larger and fancier. A heavy-duty pickup truck was parked in a barn-turned-garage off to one side. The vehicle was guarded by another man sitting cross-legged on its open tailgate. A few other people were moving around in front of the main house. All of them were dark-skinned locals carrying rifles or pistols. Most also had machetes strapped to their belts or backs.

Like the two individuals guarding the smaller house at the bottom of the hill, Cross noticed there was something off with the rest of them, too. Something about their proportions . . .

"Oh my God," Cross murmured. "They're all kids."

Cross felt sick to his stomach. He had long feared coming into contact with child soldiers, so he'd done more than his fair share of research. In Africa alone, nearly 150,000 child soldiers had been trained to use weapons and wage war. Many were orphans whose families had been destroyed by disease or violence. Many were sold by their parents in order to pay debts or simply escape poverty. Many were kidnapped and forced to fight for their captors' ideals. Many were tricked by villainous recruiters trying to find fighters however they could.

In short, the reasons children found themselves at war all across Africa were every bit as varied as the types of conflicts that robbed them of their innocence.

International law prohibited children from participating in combat, but those rules meant little to men looking to kill their rivals in pursuit of more power. If a child could hold a gun and do as he was told, such men reasoned, a child could fight for their cause. A child could kill the enemy. A child could die so that a more valuable, trained, and adult soldier didn't have to.

Sickening, Cross thought.

Cross feared that he was facing an entire camp filled with armed child soldiers. When Lancaster linked the image feed from Four-Eyes' camera to Cross's datapad, his fears were confirmed. It nearly knocked the wind out of him.

Cross looked up from his datapad at last to find Paxton staring at him. The Green Beret's jaw was set in stone. His eyes flickered between concern for Cross and rage at the sight of children carrying firearms.

"What's the play?" he asked through clenched teeth.

Cross forced himself to take a deep breath. Then another. "Evidence suggests that any survivors who made it off that plane are down there under guard," he said. "We need to confirm that."

"And when we do?" Rodgers asked. He still had his datapad playing Four-Eyes' images. Everyone did.

"We get them back," Cross said. "We go in and we get them out."

"How?" Rodgers asked.

"Quietly," Cross said. "Full black. Absolutely no contact or combat."

"That's a fine thing to say, Commander," Rodgers said in his most reasonable tone. "But those kids are all over the place down there. They're not going to be predictable like real soldiers. We don't even know how many more of them there are."

"It doesn't matter," Cross said. "No contact."

"Think this through, Commander," Rodgers insisted. His tone was patient, almost fatherly. "We can try to keep out of sight, but that might not be possible."

"It better be," Cross growled.

Rodgers' eyebrows came together as he frowned. "There's a lot of open ground down there and too many unknown variables. We can't just go down there hoping things work out for the best. What if some of our people are too injured to sneak them out? What if, by some chance, one of those kids just so happens to spot one of us and draws a weapon? A bullet does the same damage regardless of how old the person pulling the trigger is."

"We're not treating kids as hostiles," Cross said. "This is not a raid. We will not engage them."

"What if it's us or them?" Rodgers asked.

"Then withdraw. Pull back," Cross said.

"And if we can't do that?" Rodgers said, his voice rising. "I'm telling you right now, Commander, if it comes down to it, I don't care how old they are. If one of them raises a weapon and means to use it, I'm going to do what I've been trained to do —"

WHAM!

The next thing Cross knew, Rodgers was on his knees in the dirt. Cross glanced around and realized Paxton had stepped in and floored Rodgers with a hard punch.

"You've been trained to follow orders, Rodgers," Paxton said. "That's what you're going to do. Got it?"

It took a moment for Rodgers' eyes to focus. At first he simply glared up at Paxton in silent fury. But as the momentary surprise and pain faded, his reasoning returned. His eyes flicked from Paxton to

Cross and to the other team members. Everyone was either staring at Paxton in shock, glaring coldly at Rodgers, or looking expectantly at Cross.

"I read you," Rodgers finally said. He gave his head a quick shake to clear it. "And ouch."

"Get up," Cross said. The anger had vanished from his face. Only a cold, unreadable expression remained.

Paxton extended a hand down to Rodgers. Rodgers took it and hauled himself upright. When he stood, he glared at Cross without a word then walked away, putting the rest of the team between himself and his commander.

For a long time, no one spoke.

"All right," Cross said at last. "Here's the play." He looked at Yamashita then at Williams. "You two are with me. We'll make our way down and confirm whether our people are here. If so, we'll assess their condition and see about getting them out and back up here."

"Sir," Yamashita and the medic said.

Next Cross looked at Paxton, Rodgers, and Jannati. "You three, I want you to move around the site to where the road comes out the other side. Watch for anyone approaching from that side."

"Sir," Paxton and Jannati said.

Rodgers nodded but remained silent.

"You two stay here," Cross said to Lancaster and Shepherd. "Let us know if anyone tries to come in behind us." He glanced back at Lancaster. "And call the Wraith. Make sure the pilot's on his way back and knows where to look for us."

"Sir," Lancaster and Shepherd said.

"Let's move."

INTEL

DECRYPTING

IIIII IIII   II II III IIIII IIII I

12345

COM CHATTER

- AK-47: inexpensive, gas-operated assault rifle

- PING: send a digital message to a computer device

- M4 CARBINE: short and light assault rifle

3245.98 ● ● ●

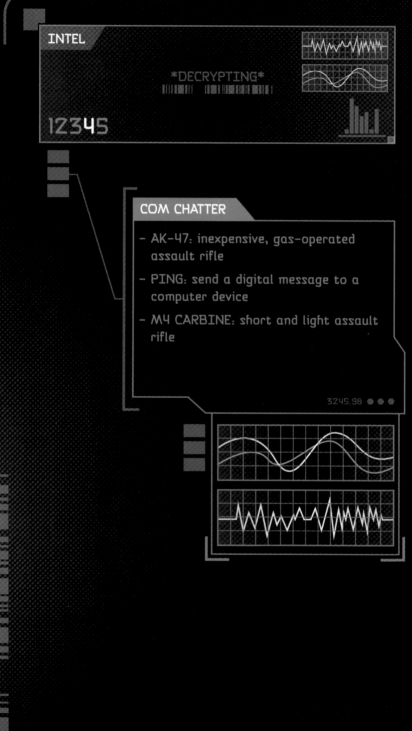

FRIENDLIES

Cross, Yamashita, and Williams made their way downhill toward the smaller house where Four-Eyes' thermal camera showed the greatest concentration of heat signatures. They made good time across the back of the coffee plantation field since the darkness and the shrubs provided some cover.

But once they reached the end of the field, only open ground lay between them and the house. The total lack of cover forced them to lie flat like worms and painstakingly inch their way along.

The open distance from the coffee shrubs to the

rear of the lower house was only a few hundred feet, but traversing it took them longer than the rest of their trip.

The three-man team finally reached a window at the rear of the house. Cross signaled to Yamashita and Williams to stop.

Cross went the rest of the way alone. He inched right up to the base of the house and rose silently to the bottom of the window. Finding it locked, he opened his tactical knife.

SNICK!

Cross used its slim blade to slide open the latch. With that done, he raised the window, inch by inch, until he was able to climb through.

Cross peeked through the musty curtain then crawled inside. He found himself in a bathroom with a scummy linoleum floor and a huge mirror on one wall. The light fixtures above were black along the bottom, filled with dead insects. The room smelled extremely unclean.

Cross was glad the toilet lid was closed.

Reaching one hand out the window, Cross signaled to Yamashita and Williams. They carefully advanced across the last bit of open ground.

Yamashita remained outside by the corner of the house to keep an eye on things as Cross helped Williams through the window.

"Commander, two kids on bicycles just sped past our position," Paxton reported via canalphone. "We weren't the ones who spooked them, but they looked scared. They're heading up the hill to the big house right now."

Cross forced himself to remain calm. Where had these newcomers come from? Why were they in such a hurry?

"Can you give me a ping if you're at the house?" Paxton asked.

CLICK!

Cross tapped his canalphone once. "Any contact with our people?" he asked.

Cross waited.

"Got it," Paxton said. "We have eyes on the hill. If anybody starts coming down your way, we'll let you know. Out."

Cross took a deep, calming breath. The alarm hadn't been raised. The mission wasn't blown. Not yet, anyway.

With a silent signal to Williams, Cross moved to one of the room's two doors. A sliver of light from the next room was visible beneath the door.

Slowly and silently, Cross produced a slim fiberscope from a pouch on his belt and plugged one end into his datapad. The other end had a flexible fiber-optic camera at the tip. Cross fed the camera beneath the door and tilted it up like a snake's head in the next room. Silently, he swept it back and forth to get a look around.

What he saw displayed on his datapad's screen gave him the first thrill of hope he'd felt since finding the crash site. In the very next room sat eight weary and disheveled US citizens, the missing Secretary of State among them.

All of them were haggard and dirty. More than a few of them wore makeshift bandages. But they were all alive. And none of them were bound at the wrists or ankles, which was more good news. Nor was there a guard in the room with them. They were likely locked inside, but it didn't appear they were being abused or tortured.

"Commander, those kids on the bikes have stirred up an awful lot of activity," Paxton reported uneasily. "More kids are coming out of the big house and forming ranks. There's a lot of confusion out there. They're starting up the truck and handing out weapons. Can you give me a ping if you've found any of our people?"

Cross tapped his canalphone once in the affirmative.

"How about the VIP?" Paxton asked.

Cross tapped once again.

"You might not have much time to get them out," Paxton said. "Do you have an exit strategy?"

Cross tapped once more.

"We'll keep you posted," Paxton replied, though he sounded doubtful. "Just hurry, sir. Out."

Cross put away the fiberscope and motioned for Williams to step back. He gently opened the door an inch to peer into the dimly lit room, then opened it just enough to slide through when no one was looking.

Cross was halfway across the room when someone realized he was there. The first to spot them was a woman lying on her back with her elbow draped over her forehead. Her eyes widened in surprise when he entered her field of vision. As her mouth opened, Cross gently covered it with his gloved hand.

Next Cross made eye contact with a man across the room who'd been sitting next to the Secretary. With a wink, Cross put the barrel of his M4 to his lips and whispered a breath-quiet "Shh." The man's eyes bulged. He nudged the Secretary of State in the ribs. The Secretary put on his best poker face and fixed his

eyes on Cross with a steady gaze. He raised a calming hand to the man on his other side, who'd only just looked up and noticed the two soldiers entering the room.

"Etes-vous Français?" the Secretary said, barely above a whisper.

"No sir, Mister Secretary," Cross replied just as quietly. He took his hand off the woman's mouth and stood up. He moved over to the Secretary and extended a hand to help him up. The Secretary took it and rose. "You're a long way from where you're supposed to be, sir."

"No good deed goes unpunished," the Secretary said with a smirk. He glanced at Williams, who had begun to wake and hush those who'd been sleeping. "I suppose you're here to take us home."

Cross nodded. "Is anybody here too hurt to move on their own?"

"We were the lucky ones," the Secretary whispered sadly. "We're tired, but we can follow your lead out of here."

"Commander, you've got incoming," Paxton said suddenly. "One of the kids is moving down the hill. He's armed. He's coming fast."

"We'll deal with it," Cross replied. "Out." He looked at Williams and pointed at the wall beside the door that led into the hallway. Williams nodded once and moved into position there.

"Deal with what?" the Secretary asked.

At that moment, raised voices were heard from outside. Whoever Paxton had seen coming down the hill had arrived at the house and was saying something to the child guards outside. Three voices rose in pitch. Cross couldn't tell if they were excited or panicked.

"Things might be about to get dicey, Mister Secretary," Cross said, making an effort to keep his voice neutral.

"What does that —"

SLAM!

Before the Secretary could finish his sentence, the door to the room swung open. A boy no older than twelve burst in. He wore denim shorts and the ragged shirt of a policeman's uniform sized for an adult. His shoes were made of old, cracked leather and laced with twine. Slung across the front of his body was a black AK-47 rifle with a rusty bayonet attached to the front. Except for the shoes, everything was too big on the scrawny, wide-eyed boy.

The boy's glance scanned from the Secretary over to Cross. When he did, his eyes seemed to go blank for a second. But then his hands went for his gun. Without so much as blinking, he hefted the comically oversized weapon and pointed it at Cross's chest.

Cross instinctively snapped his M4 carbine up to one shoulder and took aim. Only a herculean effort of will allowed him to override his training and not pull the trigger. The boy hesitated as well, but now he and Cross were locked in a stalemate. If the boy raised his voice, that stalemate would change the situation entirely.

Williams chose that moment to step out from the

shadows behind the door. With a sudden grab and a twist from the hip, he yanked the kid off his feet and pinned him on the floor.

WHUMP!

When the boy was down on his back, Williams covered his mouth with one gloved hand and snatched the rifle away with the other. Cross stepped up at the same time to look down at the kid over Williams' shoulder.

"What do you think you're doing?" the Secretary of State said. He pushed up next to Cross as one of the other civilians casually closed the door. "Let go of him. He's just a boy. They all are. And they've been trying to help us for two days."

"Come again?" Cross said.

The Secretary sighed. "When our plane went down, it was these kids who got to us first. They were looking for salvage, but the one in charge didn't want to just leave us out there to die. They said they'd take us to their commanders in exchange for the food and medical supplies we were carrying."

Food and medical supplies, Cross realized. That explained what the Secretary and the others had been doing with their plane, at least. It didn't explain the secrecy, but this wasn't the time for that line of questioning.

"Where are their commanders?" Cross asked. "Are there any adults here?"

The Secretary shook his head. "The men all went east a week ago to try to stop the rebel militias from sweeping through this area and driving everybody away. They set this place up as a guard post and left the kids in charge of it. We've been waiting for days for the adults to get back with a radio so we could call out for a rescue. None of our phones made it through the crash."

"Well, your rescue's here," Cross said. "And it's time to go."

"We'll see," the Secretary said. "Let him up."

Williams released the boy after a nod from Cross,

but he didn't give him back his rifle. One of the other civilians had picked it up and was holding it by the barrel like it was a golf club.

As soon as he was free, the boy walked up to the Secretary and began to chatter rapidly in a language Cross didn't understand. It was probably Sango, the Central African Republic's primary language, but Cross couldn't be sure.

Chief Walker probably would've known, Cross thought. *Chief Walker probably spoke it like a native. The Chief was a genius with languages.*

In that moment, Cross missed Chief Walker more than ever.

"Slow down," the Secretary said. "Slow down. Parler français."

The boy was panting. He calmed himself, then started over in French so that the Secretary and Cross's people could follow him.

The boy had been coming to deliver a warning, it turned out. Messengers — the two on bikes that Paxton had seen — had just arrived. They'd barely

escaped a disastrous battle against anti-balaka fighters. Most of the grown soldiers who'd left the children behind had been killed or scattered into the bush. The rebel militia forces would arrive to storm the coffee plantation by dawn. The older boys were waking everyone up and trying to get them ready to fight.

"How many are coming?" Cross asked the boy in French.

"They said hundreds," the boy replied in French, "but they were scared. Who knows how many, really? Enough."

"How many people do you have here?" the Secretary asked before Cross could.

"Twenty," the boy said. "Not enough."

"How many guns?" Cross asked.

The boy laughed. The cynical, bitter tone of that laugh made Cross's stomach turn. "Guns? Plenty of guns, but don't ask me about bullets. We've got enough left for one clip each. The commander took everything else. Now he's probably dead."

Cross could barely respond. Hearing a child talk like that was just wrong. Unnatural.

"Twenty guns with one clip each . . ." the Secretary mused in English. "That isn't going to hold off hundreds for very long, is it?"

"Disciplined soldiers could make a decent go of it," Cross said. "But a bunch of undertrained, sleep-deprived kids? Not a chance."

"And how many disciplined soldiers did you bring?" the Secretary asked.

"Not enough," Cross said without conviction. "But that's not our mission. Getting you people out of here is our primary concern."

The Secretary narrowed his eyes. "I was in the Special Forces. I know how things work. I'm the primary objective, and these others are secondary. Those are your orders, aren't they?"

Cross reluctantly nodded.

"Well, I'm fourth in line to run this country after the President," the Secretary said. "So let's assume I outrank whoever gave you those orders."

"If that were the case," Cross said, "what would your new orders be, sir?"

"I'd order you and your men to do everything in your power to make sure these kids don't get massacred," the Secretary said.

"To be honest, sir," Cross said, "I'm not sure Command would agree about how much authority you have over soldiers in the field."

The Secretary heaved a theatrical sigh, but he grinned just the same. "Son, would it help if I told you I play basketball with the man who gives out the Medals of Honor?"

INTEL

DECRYPTING

12345

COM CHATTER

- M240L: lighter weight version of a powerful machine gun
- M79: portable rocket-propelled grenade launcher
- MACHETE: large, heavy knife used to clear brush or sometimes as a weapon
- MILITIA: an independent, armed group of citizens

3245.98 ● ● ●

CHAPTER FIVE

PEACEKEEPER

1324.014

When the rebel militia arrived at the coffee plantation, they gave every appearance of a modern-day barbarian horde. With the sun still clinging to the horizon, they came roaring out of the forest and onto the rolling hills riding motorcycles and old pickup trucks. Their uniforms were mismatched, as were their weapons. Some had pistols, some had rifles. A handful waved torches. A few even held machetes.

They hollered and howled as they approached, the sound carrying even above the roar of their engines. Their spirits were high, likely heightened by

previous victories and the promise of one more quick victory to come.

What they found, however, was not cause for celebration. Rather than meeting a cringing, inferior foe or even a moderately armed resistance, they found only silence and calm.

They swarmed into the smaller house at the bottom of the hill, then came right back out again. Some of them tried to set it ablaze with their torches while others moved toward the coffee shrubs to do the same to the fields, but hard words in Sango stopped them. Their leader, a leathery scrap of a man with a patch over one eye, was upset. He climbed down from the truck he'd rode in on and began to lead his men on foot toward the larger house.

Within, Cross waited, watching the militia's advance through a downstairs window. The Secretary of State waited beside him on one side, Lancaster on the other. Yamashita had moved off to a nearby hillside and now lay prone, sighting down on the invaders with his M110 sniper rifle. Shepherd lay behind his M240L machine gun in cover beside the pickup truck in the shadows of the carport. Paxton and Rodgers had firing positions inside the house from second-story windows. Jannati watched the back of the house in case someone tried to sneak around that way. Williams stood guard behind the cellar door.

Down in the cellar, the American civilians and the child soldiers waited together. The former had been quite willing to hide down there from the oncoming confrontation, except for the Secretary of State.

The children, however, had been another story. The eldest insisted they should be allowed to fight. Cross sensed they were eager for revenge and wanted to take care of themselves. At first, the youngest ones had seemed willing to go along with the adults into the cellar. When their older peers tried to insist on fighting, they changed their minds. Cross had been forced to waste precious minutes arguing with all of them.

In the end, Cross had gotten them to go along with his orders only by leaving them their guns and ordering them to protect the civilians. He'd also promised them that if things turned ugly when the opposing forces arrived, he would call the children up as a reserve and give them their chance to fight.

Cross felt guilty for lying to them, but he had no intention whatsoever of putting them in harm's way. Not if he wanted to be able to look at himself in the mirror ever again. He just hoped that the plan he'd devised to protect these kids and the civilians would get the job done.

Hoping he'd made the right decision, Cross took a deep breath and nodded to Lancaster. "Here we go," he said.

The one-eyed militia leader led his men up the hill with a certain swagger. His confidence probably came from the M79 single-shot grenade launcher he held over his shoulder.

When the man got to the spot where Cross wanted him, Lancaster activated Four-Eyes and brought it to a stable, silent hover between the house and those approaching it. The fighters didn't see it until she activated its external LED lights.

The tiny diodes' lights reflected off a concave

internal mirror and shined surprisingly bright in the pre-dawn twilight.

The militia leader actually stopped and raised a hand to shield his one good eye from the harsh glare. The surprise on his face, as seen on Cross's datapad, was clear.

Capitalizing on the momentary pause, Cross tapped an icon on the datapad that synced his canalphone with the device. "That's far enough," he said in French.

When Cross spoke, Four-Eyes broadcasted his voice at megaphone volume. The bright light and the sudden booming sound made all of the soldiers group up.

The one-eyed leader cocked his head. His expression was wary but also grimly amused.

"This is what's going to happen," Cross continued in French. "Whichever one of you is in charge is going to order the rest of your men to turn around and leave this property. You can keep your weapons and your vehicles, but you're going to leave. Now."

The man with the eye patch stepped forward and scowled at Four-Eyes. "Who is this?" he barked, also in French. "French? Foreign Legion? UN peacekeepers? You don't belong here."

Cross didn't respond.

"This is a hideout for a criminal militia that's been terrorizing this area, Peacekeeper," the man announced. "We know that their forces are hiding in there. Stay out of our way so we can clean them out."

"The only people hiding in here are children and civilians," Cross replied.

"And you," the leader said.

"Listen to me," Cross said. "I said there are children here. Children who just want to go back home. To their parents."

The man with the eye patch laughed. "You haven't been in this country very long, have you, Peacekeeper?" he asked. "None of us have homes to go back to. Us because of them, them because of us. And just because those in there with you are children doesn't mean they aren't also fighters and criminals.

It doesn't mean they haven't shed our blood, just as we have shed theirs."

"They're children," Cross said one last time. "I don't want this to turn ugly, but I'm not going to let anything happen to them. I'm giving you a chance here. Take your men and go, or you're going to find out whether I'm a peacemaker or a warlord."

The hard edge in Cross's last words sent a ripple through the soldiers who understood him. They murmured and shifted their feet, fiddling with their weapons uncertainly. The confidence was still firmly in place on their leader's face, though.

"Only cowards try to negotiate with their faces hidden, Peacekeeper," the leader said.

For a moment no one said or did anything. "Commander?" Yamashita said in Cross's canalphone. "Orders?"

"Take the house!" the leader shouted to his men just then. He raised his grenade-launcher to his shoulder and flipped up the leaf sight to take aim. "Bring me this peacekeeper's head on a —"

"Do it," Cross said to Yamashita.

FWIP!

A split-second after the words left Cross's mouth, the man with the eye-patch jerked and collapsed in a boneless heap, leaving only a mist of blood blossoming in the air where he'd been standing. Thanks to the sound and flash suppression of Yamashita's barrel, no one had heard the shot or seen where it had come from.

"Who is second-in-command?" Cross barked, broadcasting through Four-Eyes again. The anger in his voice made the air go cold.

The soldiers in the front rank stared in horror at their fallen leader. A couple of them were boys not much older than the ones under Cross's protection. Some farther back were younger still.

"Someone step up," Cross ordered.

It took a moment, but one of the older men gathered his courage and came forward. In Four-

Eyes' LED glare, Cross could see he was splattered by the blood of his fallen leader.

"Good," Cross said. "You speak French?"

The man nodded.

"Then listen up," Cross said, emphasizing each syllable. "Take. Your. Men. And. Leave."

The man hesitated. "Nobody else has to die today," Cross said.

Still the man said nothing, so Cross pressed him. "Think about it. Even if you win, what do you get? How many of your own people are you willing to sacrifice just for the chance to kill a bunch of helpless children?"

The new leader wiped some of his predecessor's blood off his neck. When he didn't respond, someone farther back in the mob shouted something to him.

The words were in Sango, which Cross didn't understand, but the tone of it was clear enough. The militia men were angry. They wanted blood.

Fortunately none of them had the courage or charisma to get the attack rolling themselves. Yet.

"Do you really have children inside?" the new man in charge finally asked.

"Yes," Cross told him.

"Do you really think I won't order my soldiers to kill them?"

"Yes," Cross said again.

"Then you're using them as human shields," the leader said smugly, obviously very proud of himself. "Some might call that the act of a desperate coward, Peacekeeper."

Cross clenched his teeth. This was getting him nowhere.

"I have nothing against cowards," the man said. "In fact, I'll give you and your fellow peacekeepers a coward's choice. Come out where we can see you and lay down your weapons. If you do, my men will let you walk away with your lives. And then we will finish our business here the way it was meant to be finished."

"Absolutely not," Cross growled.

"If you had the weapons or the soldiers to do battle with us," the leader said smugly, "you would've used them already instead of trying to negotiate."

"This negotiation was for your benefit," Cross cut in. "This is your last chance. Leave. Now."

The man took a step forward. "No."

Cross sighed. "You were warned," he said.

Cross cut the transmission to Four-Eyes and switched channels. "They had their chance," he told his team. "Fire away."

As the sun's first rays broke over the horizon, a lance of fire shrieked out of the western sky and into the longhouse at the bottom of the hill.

KABOOOOOM!

The empty structure exploded in a ball of fire, courtesy of a Hellfire missile launched from the Wraith. Having introduced itself, the helicopter put its nose down and rushed toward the hilltop.

As it came on, it unfolded two M-134 miniguns from hidden compartments on its belly. For effect, the Wraith laid down two tight, laser-accurate streams of 7.62x51mm NATO rounds into the ground between the house and the militiamen.

WHIR-A-WHIR-A-WHIR.

RAT-A-TAT-TAT!

BA-BANG!

The explosion, the eerie cry of the Wraith's rotors, and the high roar of the miniguns all had the desired effect on the soldiers: terror shivered through their ranks. Adding to the swelling confusion, Shepherd opened up with his machine gun from concealment.

CHIT-CHIT-CHIT-CHIT-CHIT-CHIT-CHIT-CHIT-CHIT-CHIT-CHIT-CHIT-CHIT-CHIT-CHIT

Shepherd chewed up a handful of the vehicles that had brought the men there.

Inside the house, Lancaster aimed her M4 out

the window. Rodgers and Paxton did the same from upstairs. Atop the faraway hill, Yamashita scanned the mob for fighters who tried to rush the house or to take aim up at the Wraith. A few did the latter, firing wildly, before one of the four spotters took them down.

For the most part, though, the surprise attack had done the job exactly as Cross had intended. The militia's fighting spirit was broken.

Mere seconds later, the mob was in complete disarray. The Wraith flew back and forth over the crowd, squeezing off short streams of fire from its miniguns solely to herd the mass of them away in the same direction. The officer flying the helicopter chased the invaders half a mile back into the bush before he broke off to come back. From the sound of his voice as he reported in, he was having a great time doing it.

Cross's voice was much more serious, however. "Report," he said through the canalphone, addressing every member of his team.

"Back's clear," Jannati said.

"Front's clear," Yamashita said.

"The trucks are scrap," Shepherd said. "A few of the motorcycles got away."

"Four-Eyes took a hit," Lancaster said. "It's down."

"Everyone's fine down here," Williams said from the cellar doorway. "They want to know if they can come out."

"Not yet," Cross said. "What about casualties?"

"The militia's leader is down," Paxton said. "Both of them. All told, it looks like eight confirmed kills."

"That isn't what I'm asking," Cross said.

Before the militia had arrived, Cross had given strict orders on the off chance that they had children in their ranks. To his nauseated disappointment, he'd seen through Four-Eyes' camera that the militia had quite a few child soldiers. Now he needed to know if his people had followed his orders.

"No kids," Rodgers said. "We didn't shoot any of the kids, sir."

Cross let out a ragged breath and sat down on

the floor in a heap. "Good work, everyone," he murmured.

* * *

A week later, the team was back home. The Secretary of State was safely back in Washington, likely getting a lecture from the President. The other US civilians who'd been with him were back where they belonged as well, sulking in the knowledge that their careers in the US diplomatic corps were pretty much over. Even the bodies of those killed in the plane crash had been recovered and returned home for burial.

Getting everyone home had taken a lot of quick hopping back and forth across national borders in the Wraith, but Lancaster had coordinated it all as easy as breathing.

The most difficult problem had been what to do about the child soldiers Shadow Squadron had gone to such lengths to protect. The youngest ones who'd been at the coffee plantation the least amount of time wanted nothing more than to go home. Once the American civilians were away, Cross and Shadow

Squadron were only too willing to see the kids safely back to the refugee camps and villages they'd been taken from.

The children who had no homes to go back to presented a trickier problem. Many were orphans taken in by the militia when their homes had been destroyed. Others belonged to parents who'd fled the fighting without them. Some were just too young and had been moved around so much that they had no idea how to get back home, or even where home was.

For those lost boys, the best Cross could do was arrange transportation to one of the UN outposts in the region that specialized in deprogramming child soldiers and reintegrating them back into society. It wasn't home, and it never would be. But it was the best chance Cross saw of giving the boys a shot at having a normal life — and a future.

Sadly, not all of the child soldiers Cross had protected could be saved. Many of them disappeared into the bush the first chance they got. They took their rifles and machetes with them, likely seeking revenge on those who'd attacked them. Others went with Shadow Squadron to the camps and villages they were able to find, but only to help escort the youngest ones to safety. With that done, they admitted that they were going back out to continue the fight as soon as Cross and his men were gone.

Cross did his best to convince those who'd listen to stay home and take care of their families, but he feared most of his words fell on deaf ears. Many who lived there saw no other way to take care of their valued possessions and loved ones. For all he might want things to be different, there was only so much Cross could do.

But one thing Cross vowed to do was keep reminding the Secretary of State of what they'd seen and been through together. He would pressure him to exert what influence he could to change things through diplomatic channels. The Secretary owed those kids and all the ones who would inevitably follow in their footsteps at least that much.

Now that the Central African Republic was a world away, Cross had an internal matter to deal with. He checked his watch. *Right on time*, Cross thought. "Come in," he called.

Rodgers entered. The gunnery sergeant closed the door behind him and sat in the empty chair opposite Cross's desk. Rodgers' face was blank, but Cross could tell that the frown on his own face had been noticed.

"I know why you wanted to see me, Commander," Rodgers said. "I want you to know I talked to Sergeant Paxton after we got back. I didn't much like getting sucker punched in front of everybody, but I get where he was coming from. I told him so and said there's no hard feelings. He's assured me of the same. I don't know if he's talked to you about this yet, but I just want you to know that you're not going to have to worry about there being a problem between us."

"You're off the team," Cross said flatly.

Rodgers' expression matched the one he'd worn when Paxton punched him. "What?" he stammered.

"Your civvies and personal effects are being shipped to your next post," Cross said. "When you leave this room, you're to report to Hangar Two immediately. You'll be given your new assignment by the chief of the flight crew of the MC-130J Commando II waiting for you there."

"What is this?" Rodgers demanded. "You can't do this. Not because of one little misunderstanding."

"I have the final say about who's on my team," Cross corrected him. "And I say you're out."

"With a service record like mine, that's nuts," Rodgers argued. "And I've spent weeks training with this team . . ."

"You're a fine soldier, no doubt," Cross said. "Your skills will be appreciated wherever you end up."

"But why?" Rodgers said. He leaned forward and grabbed the edge of Cross's desk, his eyes imploring. "I thought we were friends."

Cross sighed. "Heath, I like you," he said. "You're one of the finest soldiers I've served with. That's why you're not going to be spending the rest of your career babysitting scientists in Antarctica. But you failed a test in the CAR and made me realize I misjudged you. Now I've seen what kind of soldier you really are, and it's not the kind I want on my team."

"Well, I'm sorry, Commander," Rodgers spat sarcastically, "but there are people out there who happen to want to kill us. Sometimes, whether we like it or not, we have to do distasteful things to stop that happening. Forgive me for being a realist instead of an angel."

"I don't expect my soldiers to be angels," Cross said, "but I expect them to try to be. I expect them to want to be. I thought that's who you were, but I was wrong. So we're done." He stood up, signaling that this little chat was over.

"You're making a big mistake," Rodgers said, his face twisted. He stood too, nearly knocking his chair over. "Command is going to hear about this."

"You're dismissed, Gunnery Sergeant," Cross said.

Without another word or so much as a salute, Rodgers spun on his heel and stormed out. This time he did knock the chair over, and he slammed the door hard enough to knock a picture off Cross's wall. Cross listened to his boots thumping down the hallway and shook his head as Rodgers barked at someone to get out of his way. When the noise had faded into the distance, Cross sat back down.

"I thought you understood," he said softly to no one at all. The truth was, he understood that Rodgers had made a mistake in Lobaye. The Marine had been prepared to do something horrible, but he'd been thinking of the safety of his team at the time. And when the time had come, he hadn't actually shot any of the child soldiers.

No, raising the possibility in the field of having to fire at armed children hadn't been the true test of Rodgers's character. While that insight had certainly proved illuminating and troubling, the true test had come and gone just now when Cross had confronted him with it.

Cross had given Rodgers a chance to show that he wanted to do better next time — to be better. But what Cross had hoped was a momentary lapse in judgment, Rodgers had proven was a deeper misguided conviction. That had sealed his fate. He liked Rodgers and would miss his skills, but the team would be better off without him.

Cross sighed and pushed the intercom button on his desk, paging Paxton's smaller office down the hall — the one that had been Chief Walker's until recently. "Adam? Rodgers failed. He's out."

"I'm sorry to hear that, Commander," Paxton replied. "After the talk we had, I was hoping he'd come around."

"Me too," Cross said. "But here we are. Could you send me your notes on the next three candidates?"

"They're on the way, sir. We can go over them when you're ready."

"Come on down," Cross told him. "I'll put a pot of coffee on."

MISSION DEBRIEFING

OPERATION

GUARDIAN ANGEL 009

PRIMARY OBJECTIVES

- Locate crash site

- Exfiltrate with any survivors

SECONDARY OBJECTIVES

x Avoid contact with locals

STATUS

2/3 COMPLETE

3245.98 ● ● ●

CROSS, RYAN

RANK: Lieutenant Commander
BRANCH: Navy Seal
PSYCH PROFILE: Team leader
of Shadow Squadron. Control
oriented and loyal, Cross insisted
on hand-picking each member of
his squad.

Rodgers will be leaving us, so we'll have to make do for a while. I don't need to spell out why Rodgers was dismissed from Shadow Squadron. It should be clear enough that he's not our kind of soldier.

In any case, this mission went well. We quickly located the crash, rescued the Secretary and his travel companions, and managed to protect the young men who took them in after the crash.

Great work, team.

— Lieutenant Commander Ryan Cross

ERROR
UNAUTHORIZED
USER MUST HAVE LEVEL 12 CLEARANCE
OR HIGHER IN ORDER TO GAIN ACCESS
TO FURTHER MISSION INFORMATION.

2019.681

CREATOR BIO(S)

AUTHOR

CARL BOWEN

Carl Bowen is a father, husband, and writer living in Lawrenceville, Georgia. He was born in Louisiana, lived briefly in England, and was raised in Georgia where he went to school. He has published a handful of novels, short stories, and comics. For Stone Arch Books, he has retold *20,000 Leagues Under the Sea*, *The Strange Case of Dr. Jekyll and Mr. Hyde*, *The Jungle Book*, *Aladdin and the Magic Lamp*, *Julius Caesar*, and *The Murders in the Rue Morgue*. He is the original author of *BMX Breakthrough* as well as the Shadow Squadron series.

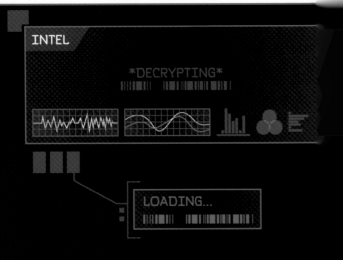

INTEL

DECRYPTING

LOADING...

WILSON TORTOSA

Wilson "Wunan" Tortosa is a Filipino comic book artist best known for his work on *Tomb Raider* and the American relaunch of *Battle of the Planets* for Top Cow Productions. Wilson attended Philippine Cultural High School, then went on to the University of Santo Tomas where he graduated with a Bachelor's Degree in Fine Arts, majoring in Advertising.

BENNY FUENTES

Benny Fuentes lives in Villahermosa, Tabasco, in Mexico, where the temperature is just as hot as the sauce. He studied graphic design in college, but now he works as a full-time illustrator in the comic book and graphic novel industry for companies like Marvel, DC Comics, and Top Cow Productions. He shares his home with two crazy cats, Chelo and Kitty, who act like they own the place.

2019.681

AUTHOR DEBRIEFING

CARL BOWEN

Q/When and why did you decide to become a writer?
A/I've enjoyed writing ever since I was in elementary
   school. I wrote as much as I could, hoping to
   become the next Lloyd Alexander or Stephen King,
   but I didn't sell my first story until I was in college.
   It had been a long wait, but the day I saw my story
   in print was one of the best days of my life.

Q/What made you decide to write *Shadow Squadron*?
A/As a kid, my heroes were always brave knights or
   noble loners who fought because it was their duty,
   not for fame or glory. I think the special ops soldiers
   of the US military embody those ideals. Their jobs
   are difficult and often thankless, so I wanted to
   show how cool their jobs are and also express my
   gratitude for our brave warriors.

Q/What inspires you to write?
A/My biggest inspiration is my family. My wife's love
   and support lifts me up when this job seems too hard
   to keep going. My son is another big inspiration.

He's three years old, and I want him to read my books and feel the same way I did when I read my favorite books as a kid. And if he happens to grow up to become an elite soldier in the US military, that would be pretty awesome, too.

Q/Describe what it was like to write these books.
A/The only military experience I have is a year I spent in the Army ROTC. It gave me a great respect for the military and its soldiers, but I quickly realized I would have made a pretty awful soldier. I recently got to test out a friend's arsenal of firearms, including a combat shotgun, an AR-15 rifle, and a Barrett M82 sniper rifle. We got to blow apart an old fax machine.

Q/What is your favorite book, movie, and game?
A/My favorite book of all time is *Don Quixote*. It's crazy and it makes me laugh. My favorite movie is either *Casablanca* or *Double Indemnity*, old black-and-white movies made before I was born. My favorite game, hands down, is *Skyrim,* in which you play a heroic dragonslayer. But not even *Skyrim* can keep me from writing more *Shadow Squadron* stories, so you won't have to wait long to read more about Ryan Cross and his team. That's a promise.

COM CHATTER

-MISSION PREVIEW: After an unknown aircraft crashes in Antarctica near a science facility, Shadow Squadron is deployed to recover the device. But when Russian special forces intervene, Cross gets caught between the mission's objective and the civilian scientists' safety.

3245.98 ● ● ●

SHADOW SQUADRON

PHANTOM SUN

CARL BOWEN

PHANTOM SUN

Cross tapped his touchscreen to start the video. On the screen, a few geologists began pointing and waving frantically. The camera watched them all for another couple of seconds then lurched around in a half circle and tilted skyward. Blurry clouds wavered in and out of focus for a second before the cameraman found what the others had been pointing at — a lance of white fire in the sky. The image focused, showing what appeared to be a meteorite with a trailing white plume behind it punching through a hole in the clouds. The camera zoomed out to allow the cameraman to better track the object's progress through the sky.

"Is that a meteorite?" Shepherd asked.

"Just keep watching," Brighton said, breathless with anticipation.

Right on cue, the supposed meteorite suddenly flared white, then changed directions in mid-flight by almost 45 degrees. Grunts and hisses of surprise filled the room.

"So . . . not a meteorite," Shepherd muttered.

The members of Shadow Squadron watched in awe as the falling object changed direction once again with another flare and then pitched downward. The camera angle twisted overhead and then lowered to track its earthward trajectory from below.

"And now . . . sonic boom," Brighton said.

The camera image shook violently for a second as the compression wave from the falling object broke the speed of sound and as the accompanying burst shook the cameraman's hands. A moment later, the object streaked into the distance and disappeared into the rolling hills of ice and snow. The video footage ended a few moments later with a still image of the

gawking geologists looking as excited as a bunch of kids on Christmas morning.

"This video popped up on the Internet a few hours ago," Cross began. "It's already starting to go viral."

"What is it?" Second Lieutenant Aram Jannati said. Jannati, the team's newest member, came from the Marine Special Operations Regiment. "I can't imagine we'd get involved if it was just a meteor."

"Meteorite," Staff Sergeant Adam Paxton corrected. "If it gets through the atmosphere to the ground, it's a meteorite."

"That wasn't a meteorite, man," Brighton said, hopping out of his chair. He dug his smartphone out of a cargo pocket and came around the table toward the front of the room. He laid his phone on the touchscreen Cross had used and then synced up the two devices. With that done, he used his phone as a remote control to run the video backward to the first time the object had changed directions. He used a slider to move the timer back and forth, showing the object's fairly sharp angle of deflection through the sky.

"Meteorites can't change directions like this," Brighton said. "This is 45 degrees of deflection at least, and the thing barely even slows down."

"I'm seeing a flare when it turns," Paxton said. "Meteors hold a lot of frozen water when they're in space. It expands when it reaches the atmosphere. If those gases are venting or exploding, couldn't that cause a change of direction?"

"Not this sharply," Brighton said before Cross could reply. "Besides, if you look at this…" He used a few swipes across his phone to pause the video and zoom in on the flying object. At the new resolution, a dark, oblong shape was visible inside a wreath of fire. He then advanced through the first and second changes of direction and tracked it a few seconds forward before pausing again. "See?"

A room full of shrugs and uncomprehending looks met Brighton's eager gaze.

"It's the same size!" Brighton said, tossing his hands up in mock frustration. "If this thing had exploded twice — and with enough force to push something this big in a different direction both times — it would be in a million pieces. So those aren't explosions. They're thrusters or something."

"Which makes this what?" Shepherd asked. "A UFO?"

"Sure," Paxton answered in a mocking tone. "It's unidentified, it's flying, and it's surely an object. It probably has little green men inside, too."

"You don't know that it doesn't," Brighton said. "I mean, this thing could be from outer space!"

"Sit down, Sergeant," Chief Walker said.

Brighton reluctantly did so, pocketing his phone.

"Don't get ahead of yourself, Ed," Cross said, retaking control of the briefing. "Phantom Cell analysts have authenticated the video and concluded that this thing isn't just a meteorite. It's some kind of metal construct, though they can't make out specifics from the quality of the video. I suppose it's possible it's from outer space, but it's much more likely it's man-made. All we know for sure is that it's not American made. Therefore, our mission is to get out to where it came down, secure it, zip it up, and bring it back for a full analysis. Any questions so far?"

"I have one," Jannati said. "What is Phantom Cell?"

Cross nodded. Jannati was the newest member of the team, and as such he wasn't as familiar with all the various secret programs. "Phantom Cell is a parallel program to ours," Cross explained. "But their focus is on psy-ops, cyberwarfare, and research and development."

Jannati nodded. "Geeks, in other words," he said. Brighton gave him a sour look but said nothing.

"What are we supposed to do about the scientists who found this thing?" Lieutenant Kimiyo Yamashita asked. True to his stoic nature, the sniper had finished his breakfast and coffee while everyone else was talking excitedly. "Do they know we're coming?"

"That's the problem," Cross said, frowning. "We haven't heard a peep out of them since this video appeared online. Attempts at contacting them have gone unanswered. Last anyone heard, the geologists who made the video were going to try to find the point of impact where this object came down. We have no idea whether they found it or not, or what happened to them."

"Isn't this how the movie *Aliens* starts?" Brighton asked. "With a space colony suddenly cutting off communication after a UFO crash landing?"

Paxton rolled his eyes. "Lost Aspen, the base there, is pretty new," he said. "And it's in the middle of Antarctica. It could just be a simple technical failure."

"You have zero imagination, man," Brighton said. "You're going to be the first one the monster eats. Well . . . after me, anyway."

"These are our orders," Cross continued as if he had never been interrupted. "Find what crashed, bring the object back for study, figure out why the research station stopped communicating, and make sure the civilians are safe. Stealth is going to be of paramount importance on this one. Nobody has any territorial claims on Marie Byrd Land, but no country is supposed to be sending troops on missions anywhere in Antarctica, either."

"Are we expecting anyone else to be breaking that rule while we are, Commander?" Yamashita asked.

"It's possible," Cross said. "If this object is man-made, whoever made it is probably going to come looking for it. Any other government that attached the same significance to the video that ours did could send people, too. No specific intel has been confirmed yet, but it's only a matter of time before someone takes an active interest."

"Seems like the longer the video's out there, the more likely we're going to have company," Yamashita said.

"About that," Cross said with a mischievous smile on his face. "Phantom Cell's running a psy-ops campaign in support of our efforts. They're simultaneously spreading the word that the video's a hoax and doing their best to stop it from spreading and to remove it from circulation."

"Good luck to them on that last one," Brighton snorted. "It's the Internet. Phantom Cell's good, but nobody's that good."

"Not our concern," Cross said. "We ship out in one hour. Get your gear on the Commando. We'll go over more mission specifics during the flight. Understood?"

"Sir," the men responded in unison. At a nod from Cross, they rose and gathered up the remains of their breakfast. As they left the briefing room, Walker remained behind. He gulped down the last of his coffee before standing up.

"Brighton's sure excited," Walker said.

"I knew he would be," Cross replied. "I didn't expect him to try to help out so much with the briefing, though."

"Is that what I'm like whenever I chip in from up here?" Walker asked.

Cross fought off the immediate urge to toy with his second-in-command, though he couldn't stop the mischievous smile from coming back. "Maybe a little bit," he said.

Walker returned Cross's grin. "Well, then I wholeheartedly apologize."